Honeysuckle Cottage
Poppy's House

Forget-Me-Not Cottage
Grandpa's House and Office

Poppy Field

N
W   E
S

Honeypot Cottage
Honey and Granny Bumble's House

Blossom
Bakehouse

Cornsilk Castle
and Courtyard

Village Hall

Sage's
Vet Surgery

Post Office

River Swan

Beehive
Beauty Salon

Barley Farm
The Meadowsweets' House

Riverside
Stables

Honeypot Hill
Railway Station

To Camomile Cove
via Periwinkle Lane

Check out Princess Poppy's brilliant website:

www.princesspoppy.com

GET WELL SOON
A PICTURE CORGI BOOK 978 0 552 55604 0

First published in Great Britain by Picture Corgi,
an imprint of Random House Children's Books
A Random House Group Company

This edition published 2008

1 3 5 7 9 10 8 6 4 2

Text copyright © Janey Louise Jones, 2008
Illustration copyright © Picture Corgi Books, 2008
Illustrations by Veronica Vasylenko
Design by Tracey Cunnell

The right of Janey Louise Jones to be identified as the author of this work has been
asserted in accordance with the Copyright, Designs and Patents Act 1988.

Picture Corgi Books are published by Random House Children's Books,
61–63 Uxbridge Road, London W5 5SA
www.princesspoppy.com
www.kidsatrandomhouse.co.uk
www.rbooks.co.uk

Addresses for companies within The Random House Group Limited
can be found at: www.randomhouse.co.uk/offices.htm

THE RANDOM HOUSE GROUP Limited Reg. No. 954009

A CIP catalogue record for this book is available from the British Library.

Printed in China

Get Well Soon

Written by Janey Louise Jones

PICTURE CORGI

Poppy was practising for her gym club competition. She loved gym and was especially good at cartwheels, but today she just couldn't get anything right because she was so worried about Grandpa. He had been taken into hospital a few days before and Poppy was missing him very much.

"The hospital just rang," called Mum as she walked into the garden. "Grandpa is well enough for visitors so we can go and see him this afternoon."

"Yippee," replied Poppy, and dashed off towards her bedroom to choose an outfit.

Nurses and doctors marched along corridors with clip boards and it seemed to Poppy that half the world must be ill.

WARD A

When they entered Grandpa's ward, they found him propped up on lots of pillows with his eyes closed. Poppy was shocked by how thin and pale he looked and didn't recognize him until she noticed his striped pyjamas.

She looked at Mum for reassurance.

"He's over the worst of it, darling. He just needs lots of rest."

"But when will he be better?" asked Poppy.

"In a week or so," replied Mum.

"A week?" exclaimed Poppy. "That's way too long!"

And at that moment they heard the faintest chuckle from Grandpa's bed. "Hello, Princess Poppy," said Grandpa softly as he opened his eyes and smiled at her. "What a lovely surprise."

Poppy sat down next to Grandpa's bed and chatted away to him about school, her friends and the gym competition. She was having such a nice time that she almost forgot he was even ill until the doctor came in and told them that he needed to rest now.

"Get well soon, Grandpa," said Poppy as she kissed him goodbye, waved her flower wand over him and made a secret wish that he would be home by the weekend.

When they got home, the phone was ringing.

"Guess what?" laughed Mum when she'd finished the call.
"That was the hospital. Grandpa is so much better that
they're going to let him come home tomorrow."

"Yippee!" said Poppy as she danced around the room.
"My wish *has* come true!"

On Sunday, Poppy changed into her best princess dress and went over to Forget-Me-Not Cottage.

When she saw Grandpa, she was so happy to have him back that she burst into tears and gave him a huge hug.

"I've missed you so much, Grandpa," said Poppy in a muffled voice.

"I've missed you too," said Grandpa. "How is my special princess? Did you win the competition?"

"No, I came LAST!"

"Never mind. It doesn't matter who wins as long as you take part. Anyway, you've been doing something much more important," said Grandpa.

"What do you mean?" asked Poppy.

"Helping me get better, of course," he smiled as he stroked Poppy's hair. "Your visits to the hospital cheered me up so much, the doctors decided to let me come home early. You may not be a gym princess but you'll always be my princess because you're so thoughtful and caring."

"Thank you, Grandpa," said Poppy, beaming with pride.